Surprise parties

Compiled by Pat Edwards

Acknowledgements

We are grateful to the following for permission to reproduce copyright material: Jonathan Cape Ltd and Harper & Row Publishers Inc. for the poem 'Magical Eraser', text and illustration from *Where The Sidewalk Ends: The Poems and Drawings of Shel Silverstein* Copyright © 1974 by Evil Eye Music; the author, Judy Delton for an extract and illustrations from *Brimhall Turns To Magic*, illustrated by Bruce Degen; Dodd Mead & Company Inc. for extracts from *Morris Has a Cold* by Bernard Wiseman, Copyright © 1978 by Bernard Wiseman; Pantheon Books, a Division of Random House Inc. for an extract from *The Surprise Party* by Annabelle Prager Copyright © 1977 by Annabelle Prager, illustrations by Tomie de Paola.

Illustrators, other than those acknowledged above, include: Jill Brierley pp.62-64; Marjory Gardner pp.4-5, 32-35; Marzia Mielli pp.52-53; Sally Strangeways pp.36-39.

Contents

PARTY WORDS

flame Flame flame Flame flame Flame flame Flame flame Flame flame Flame

candle candle candle candle candle candle candle candle

pink sticky icing pink sticky icing

pink sticky icing pink sticky icing

birthday cake birthday cake bir

paper frill paper frill paper frill p

Happy

balloon balloon balloon balloon balloon balloon balloon balloon balloon balloon balloon

paper frill paper frill paper frill pap

birthday cake birthday cake birthday c

plate plate plate plate plate plate plate plate plate plate

streamer streamer streamer streamer streamer streamer streamer streamer streamer streamer str

string string string string string string string string string

blower blower blower blower blower blower blower blower blower blower blower blower blower blower blower blower blower

4

candle candle flame flame Flame flame

candle candle flame Flame Flame flame

candle candle flame flame flame flame

candle candle flame flame Flame Flame

ribbon ribbon ribbon ribbon ribbon ribbon ribbon ribbon ribbon ribbon ribbon ribbon ribbon ribbon ribbon ribbon ribbon ribbon

present present present present present

sticky icing pink sticky icing pink sticky icing pink sticky icing pink sticky icing

straw straw straw straw straw straw straw straw straw straw straw straw straw

glass glass

present present present present present present present present present present present present present present present present present present present

ink sticky icing pink sticky icing

cake birthday cake birthday cake birthday

frill paper frill paper frill paper frill paper frill paper frill paper

Birthday

paper frill paper frill paper frill paper frill

irthday cake birthday cake birthday cake

present

plate plate plate plate plate plate plate plate plate plate plate

hat paper hat paper hat paper hat paper hat paper hat paper hat paper

paper hat paper hat paper

diamond diamond diamond diamond diamond diamond diamond diamond diamond diamond

streamer streamer streamer streamer streamer streamer streamer streamer streamer streamer streamer

paper hat paper hat paper hat paper hat paper hat

5

The Surprise party

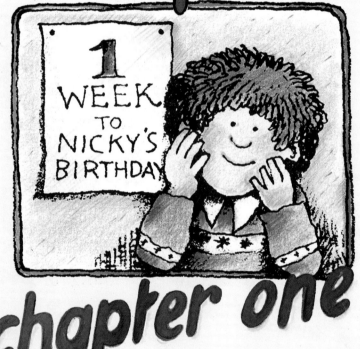

chapter one

"Know what?" said Nicky.

"No, what?" said Albert.

"My birthday is coming," said Nicky. "I am going to have a birthday party."

"Great!" said Albert. "Are you going to invite me?"

"Of course I am going to invite you," said Nicky. "I'm going to invite you and Ann, and Jenny and Jan, and Morris and Doris, and Dan."

"That sure is a lot of people," said Albert.

"You have to have a lot of people at a birthday party," said Nicky. "That way you get a lot of presents. Come on. I need you to help me."

Nicky took out his piggy bank. He shook it upside down. Out fell a few pennies.

"Oh no," he said. "This is not enough money for a party."

"What are you going to do?" said Albert.

"I'll think of something," said Nicky.

Suddenly his face broke into a smile. "I know," he said. "I'll have a surprise party."

"A surprise party for who?" asked Albert.

"A surprise party for me," said Nicky.

"You can't give a surprise party for yourself," said Albert. "You won't be surprised."

8

"Of course I can't give a surprise party for myself," said Nicky. "But YOU can. You and Ann, and Jenny and Jan, and Morris and Doris, and Dan."

"How are we going to do that?" asked Albert.

"Easy," said Nicky. "You say — Listen you guys. Nicky's birthday is coming. Let's give him a surprise party. Then they'll say — What a good idea. We love surprise parties. You can bring the cake. Ann can bring the ice-cream. Jenny can bring the . . ."

"Oh, I get it," said Albert. "Everyone will bring something for the party. What a good idea."

"You can get the party ready at my house while I am out having my tuba lesson," Nicky said. "When I come home you will yell **Surprise!**

You know, Albert, I'll be very surprised if this doesn't turn out to be the best surprise party that ever was."

chapter two

Albert ran home to call up Ann, and Jenny and Jan, and Morris and Doris, and Dan.

Sure enough, they all said, "What a good idea! We love surprise parties."

They all met at Albert's house to plan the party.

"We can fix the party at Nicky's house while he is out having his tuba lesson," Albert said. "When he comes home we will jump out and yell **Surprise!**"

Just then the telephone rang.

Albert answered it.

"Hello," he said.

It was Nicky.

"I forgot to tell you something," whispered Nicky. "I love balloons with Happy Birthday on them."

"Okay," said Albert, nervously. "Goodbye."

"Who was that?" asked Ann.

Albert thought very fast.

"Uh . . . that was my Aunt Belinda," he said. "Shall we have balloons with Happy Birthday on them?"

"Yes, yes, yes," shouted everyone.

Ting-a-ling-a-ling. The phone rang again.
Albert answered it again. It was Nicky again.

"Can we have crackers?" said Nicky. "The
kind that go bang when you pull them?"

"Sure, Aunt Belinda," said Albert. He
slammed down the phone and turned to the
group. "Shall we have crackers?" he asked.

"Do you mean the kind that go bang when
you pull them?" said Jenny. "They're so
scary. I love them."

Ting-a-ling-a-ling.

"Let me answer it," said Jan.

"No, no, no," cried Albert, grabbing the phone. It was Nicky again.

"Be sure that everyone brings a present," said Nicky. "And remember my favourite colour is blue."

"Of course, Aunt Belinda," said Albert. **"Good-bye!"**

"Why does your aunt call you every five minutes?" asked Morris and Doris.

"My Aunt Belinda is very lonely," said Albert. "Now let me think. Nicky's favourite colour is blue. I think I will make a beautiful blue birthday cake."

"Do we have to bring a present?" asked Dan.

"Everyone has to bring a present," said Albert. "Oh boy, will Nicky be surprised!"

chapter three

The next day Nicky and Albert were roller skating in the park.

"It would be awful if anyone found out that I know about the party!" said Nicky.

"Shush," said Albert. "Here comes Ann on her pogo stick."

"I'd better make sure that Ann doesn't think I know about the party," said Nicky.

Ann stopped hopping.

"Hi," she said.

"Hi, Ann," said Nicky. "Guess what I am doing on my birthday."

"What?" asked Ann. She gave Albert a worried look.

"My tuba teacher is taking me to a concert," said Nicky.

"Oh NO," said Ann.

"Why do you say Oh NO?" asked Nicky. "Don't you like concerts?"

"What I meant to say," said Ann, "was, Oh no — no kidding. Excuse me. I have to go and see Jenny and Jan, and Morris and Doris, and Dan."

Ann got on her pogo stick and hopped away as fast as she could. Nicky laughed and laughed.

"I fooled her," he said. "Now nobody can possibly think that I know about the party. Oh, I can't wait for my birthday to come."

chapter four

Three days later Nicky was walking home from his tuba lesson.

He gave a little skip of excitement because his birthday had finally come.

When Nicky got to his little house it was all dark.

He practised making a surprised face.

He opened his front door.

Nothing happened.

He went into his living room.

Nothing happened.

He turned on the light.

Nobody was there.

"Where's the party?" he wondered. "Oh, I bet they are hiding." He waited and waited. Nothing happened.

Then the doorbell rang.

"There they are!" he thought, happily. He practised making more surprised faces on the way to the door.

It was Albert, all alone.

"Where is my party?" asked Nicky.

"Oh Nicky," said Albert. "It is awful. Ann
told everyone that you were going to a
concert with your tuba teacher so they called
off the party."

Nicky sat down. "Oh my," he sighed. "Oh,
my beautiful surprise party."

A big tear ran down his cheek.

"Don't feel too bad," Albert said. "They decided to have the party on your next birthday. You can look forward to it for twelve whole months."

"I should never have played a trick on my friends," cried Nicky.

"Never mind," said Albert. "I made a cake for you anyway. Come to my house and we can eat it."

They walked to Albert's house.

Albert opened his front door.

Nicky went in.

Albert turned on the light.

"Surprise! Surprise!" shouted Ann, and Jenny and Jan, and Morris and Doris, and Dan.

Nicky looked all around him.

There were balloons with Happy Birthday on them. There was a table with a blue paper table cloth and seven blue paper plates. By each plate there was a red cracker and a little basket filled with candy.

Best of all, there was a pile of presents, seven of them, each one tied with a big bow, and each one with a surprise inside.

"Wow!" breathed Nicky.

"Know what?" said Albert.

"No, what?" said Nicky.

"You said you wanted the best surprise party that ever was. So we made it a surprise."

Story by A. Prager,
illustrated by Tomie de Paola.

HAPPY BIRTH[

WHO was Patty Hill?

She was a kindergarten teacher in the town of Louisville in the state of Kentucky in the United States of America.

WHY is she remembered?

Because she wrote a song everyone knows without having to be taught it. It's probably the best known song in the world. It's the Happy Birthday song and Patty Hill wrote it for the children in her kindergarten.

AY PATTY HILL

WHEN did she live?

From sometime around 1869 until 1946.

HOW did other people learn about Patty Hill's song?

Patty Hill was such a good teacher that other teachers and students came to her school to find out why it was such a joyful place. They took the birthday song back to their classrooms and their pupils taught it to their mums and dads . . . and soon EVERYONE knew it!

Invitation List

7 people NOT to invite to a birthday party:

1. The big bad wolf, because he might eat your grandma.

2. Georgie Porgie, because he'd kiss the girls and make them cry.

3. Wee Willie Winkie, because he'd want everyone in bed by eight o'clock.

4. Goldilocks, because she breaks chairs.

5. The Knave of Hearts, because he steals tarts.

6. The Gingerbread Man, because he wouldn't stay to be eaten.

7. Little Jack Horner, because he eats with his thumb.

Come to My Party
(Notes passed in school)

Monday

Dear Sally,
Would you like to come to my birthday party on Saturday?
Patsy

Dear Patsy,
Yes please! Who else is coming?
Sally

Dear Sally,
Only you. Patsy

Patsy

Dear Patsy, Why only me?   Sally
P.S. What would a vampire say if you offered to pull out his teeth?

Dear Sally, He'd say, "No fangs". Mum says only one friend and the family.
Patsy   Why did the sword swallower eat pins and needles?

Dear Patsy, Because he was on a diet.
How many in your family?
Sally

Dear Sally,
Me, Mum and my baby brother.   No dad.
What happened to the silk worms who had a race?
Patsy

Dear Patsy,
They ended up in a tie.
I've never been the
only one at a party
before. What will we
be doing?
Sally

Dear Sally,
We'll play hide and seek and have a
treasure hunt I think.
Careful, Miss T. is watching.   Patsy

Tuesday

Dear Lisa,
Patsy has asked me to her birthday party, but I'm the
only one and now I don't want to go. She says we'll
play hide and seek and have a treasure hunt. Big deal!
How can you do that with only two of you?
                              What can I do?
                              I've got to get out of it!!!
                                        Sally

Dear Sally,
Tell her you have to go to your
grandma's.
        Lisa   Why does a mother
                  kangaroo
                  hate rain?

Dear Lisa,
Because the kids have to play inside.
No good. I told Mum I said yes and she
said I have to keep my promise. Sally
                    Think again. Sally

Dear Sally,
Fall off the swings
and break
your leg.
        Lisa

Dear Lisa,
Ha! Ha! Very clever.
Think again. Sally

Sally

37

Wednesday

Lisa

Dear Sally,
Guess what? Timmy's got measles! Come round after school and I'll get him to breathe on you. That should stop you having to go on Sat. What's a cannibal's favourite game?
Lisa

Dear Lisa,
Swallow the leader.
Great idea!!
Sally

I've got spots

Thursday

Dear Sally,
How do you feel? Lisa

Dear Lisa,
Not even one spot!
Sally

Boo, hoo!

Friday

Dear Sally, Did you hear what happened to the butcher who backed into his meat slicer? He got a little behind in his work! Any spots yet?
Lisa

Dear Lisa,
That joke's rude!
As a measle spreader your little brother is a flop!
How do you sprain an ankle?
Sally

still no spots

Dear Sally,
Come at 2 o'clock tomorrow.
I can hardly wait.
It's going to be fun.
Patsy

Dear Patsy,
Okay. If I don't come I've either sprained my ankle or got measles.
Sally

Dear Sally,
Why would you sprain your ankle or get measles?
Is it part of a riddle?

Patsy

Dear Patsy,
Forget it. I was being funny.
Ha! Ha! Sally

Dear Sally, Try jumping off the roof. Sorry I can't be there to help. I've got recorder practice. If King Midas sat on gold, who sat on silver?

Lisa

Dear Lisa,
That idea stinks! I'll just have to go and pretend to enjoy myself. Sally
P.S. The answer is The Lone Ranger

Monday

Dear Lisa, **WOW !!** some party
What a fantastic party! It was the best I've been to **EVER!!** Sally

Dear Sally,
Well ? ? ?
What was it like?
Lisa

Sally

Dear Lisa,
It was **ABSOLUTELY FABULOUS !!** WOW

Guess what? When Patsy said she had to have just me and her family I didn't know she had hundreds of relations — well 13 cousins and 3 aunts and 7 uncles who are only in their teens. We played hide and seek all over the park and had a treasure hunt in and out of all the houses in the street (where the relations live) and a barbecue, and when it got dark they told ghost stories round a bonfire and I didn't get home till 10 o'clock and Mum was furious! It was the BEST and BIGGEST party I've ever been to.
Sally.

Magic made easy

"Bear!" called Brimhall, throwing open the front door.

Bear looked up from his book. "Brimhall, are you home from your painting class already?" he said.

"The art class was filled, Bear. They had no room for new students. I signed up for a better class. It's called 'Magic Made Easy'!"

"Why, Brimhall, that sounds exciting!" said Bear.

Brimhall whipped out a pack of cards. "Pick a card, any card, Bear."

Bear rubbed his paws together and drew a card.

Brimhall shuffled the rest. Then he looked carefully through the pack. "The card you are holding is a . . . an ace of spades!"

Bear looked at his card. "Well, you're close, Brimhall. I have the queen of hearts."

Brimhall frowned.

"You've only had one lesson, Brimhall," said Bear kindly. "These things take time."

The two cousins turned out the light and got ready for bed.

The next day Brimhall practised his card tricks some more. All week he read his magic book and tried new tricks.

After the second lesson, Brimhall came home very excited.

He was carrying a big black bag.

"Bear!" he cried. "Wait until you see this! I have something exciting to show you!"

Bear took off his apron. "Wait, Brimhall. Let me call Raccoon and Porcupine over, so they can see it, too." Bear rushed to the phone. "Come as soon as you can," he said. "Brimhall is now a magician, you know. He has learned a fine new trick. You will be the first to see it!"

While they waited for their guests, Bear and
Brimhall set three chairs in a row. They put
Bear's table up in front. Raccoon and Porcupine
rushed in, all out of breath.

"We're ready, Brimhall," said Bear.

Brimhall opened his bag and took out a large
black hat.

"You see this hat?" he asked.

The audience nodded. "Yes! Yes!" they said.

Brimhall held up the hat. "Look inside the
hat," he said. The audience looked inside.
"There is nothing inside this hat," Brimhall
declared. The audience agreed.

Brimhall put the hat down on the table. "Now I will place this large handkerchief over the hat," said Brimhall.

The audience watched closely.

"Now there must be absolute silence," Brimhall said.

No one moved a muscle. Brimhall closed his eyes and held his paws over the hat.

"*Abra-cadabra*

Kalamazoo

Here is a large

White rabbit for you!"

Brimhall opened his eyes and stuck a paw into the hat. He pulled out a large white rabbit.

Bear shouted and clapped.

"You are so clever, Brimhall!

A rabbit! From an empty hat!"

"That is amazing!" cried Raccoon.

"That is MAGIC!" said Porcupine.

The audience clapped and clapped.

Brimhall and the rabbit bowed.

"Now then," said Brimhall, "I will make the rabbit disappear!"

Brimhall picked the rabbit up, put him back in the hat, and covered him with the handkerchief.

"Abra-cadabra

Kalamazoo

Make this rabbit

Vanish from view!"

Brimhall opened his eyes. The rabbit was still in the hat.

The audience could see his white ears sticking out the top.

"I must have made a little mistake," said Brimhall. "I will try again." Brimhall held his paws over the hat. He closed his eyes and thought hard.

"Abra-cadabra

Ginger beer.

Now may this rabbit

At once disappear!"

Brimhall opened his eyes. The rabbit was still in the hat.

The rabbit stretched. He yawned. The audience waited politely.

Brimhall walked around the hat. He looked under the table and up at the ceiling. "Ah," he said. "I believe I know what the problem is."

"Good," said the rabbit, pulling his ears into the hat.

Bear and Porcupine and Raccoon crossed their paws for luck.

"Abra-cadabra

Ziz boom bam.

Disappear, Rabbit —

I tell you to scram!"

"I've had enough," said the rabbit, climbing out of the hat. "My legs are stiff."

Brimhall got out his magic book. The rabbit came over to Porcupine and Raccoon.

"My name is Roger," he said, shaking their paws. "I don't usually have time between magic acts to meet anyone. But with *this* magician" — Roger looked at Brimhall — "I may be here a while."

"I will make you a bed on the sofa, Roger," said Bear. Brimhall was still reading.

"Well, we had better be going," said Raccoon and Porcupine. "Thank you for the magic show, Brimhall."

Brimhall was muttering magic words to himself.

"Brimhall," said Bear, "don't feel so bad. You did pull a rabbit out of a hat. I don't know anyone who can do that."

"Still," said Brimhall, "a rabbit that you pull out of a hat is SUPPOSED to disappear. I must be saying the wrong magic words."

Brimhall shut his book. "I will try again tomorrow."

"I say," said Roger, "can you lend me some pyjamas? I don't happen to have mine with me."

"Dear me," said Bear. "I don't believe I have anything to fit you. Brimhall, do you have anything to fit Roger?"

"I have a large muffler," said Brimhall. "It should be just right."

Roger wrapped himself in Brimhall's muffler and lay down on the sofa.

Soon all three animals were sound asleep.

Story by Judy Delton,
illustrated by Bruce Degen.

Thumb Trick!

Want to scare a friend by making her think she has pulled your thumb off?

You need two things:

1 a handkerchief
2 a piece of raw carrot
   the same size as your thumb.

Hide the piece of carrot in your hand. Tell your friend you are going to amaze her with a magic trick. Throw the handkerchief over your hand, then let the carrot poke out as if it is your thumb. Say to your friend, "Now, hold my thumb tightly." When she does, pull your hand away. Hide your thumb in your fist and hold it up, shouting, "Help! You've pulled off my thumb!"

Magical Eraser

She wouldn't believe
This pencil has
A magical eraser.
She said I was a silly moo,
She said I was a liar too,
She dared me prove that it was true,
And so what could I do —
I erased her!

Shel Silverstein

Morris
Has a Cold

Story and illustrations by
Bernard Wiseman

Morris the Moose said, "I have a cold. My nose is walking."

Boris the Bear said, "You mean your nose is running."

"No," said Morris. "My nose is walking. I only have a little cold."

Boris said, "Let me feel your forehead."

Morris said, "Four heads! I don't have four heads!"

Boris said, "I know you don't have four heads. But this is called your forehead."

Morris said, "That is my ONE head."

"All right," Boris growled. "Let me feel your one head."

Boris put his hand on Morris's forehead.

Boris said, "Your one head feels hot. That means you are sick. You should lie down."

Morris lay down.

"Not HERE!" Boris shouted. "You are sick. You should lie down on a bed. Here is a bed. Come lie down. Put these covers on."

"No, no," said Boris. "Do not cover ALL of you. Why did you cover your head?"

Morris said, "Because my head has the cold."

Boris said, "Your head should not be covered."

Boris took the covers from Morris's head.

"…**A-CHOO** " Morris let out a big sneeze.

Boris covered Morris's head.

Boris asked, "How does your throat feel?"

Morris said, "Hairy."

"No, no," said Boris. "I don't mean outside. How does your throat feel INSIDE?"

Morris opened his mouth to feel
the inside of his throat.

"No! No! No!" Boris shouted.
"Oh — just open your mouth. Let me look inside."

Boris said, "Your throat is red.
I know what is good for it. I will make you
some hot tea."

"Hot what?" asked Morris.

Boris said, "TEA. Don't you know
what tea is?"

"Yes," said Morris, "I know what it is.
T is like *A, B, C, D* . . ."

"No! No!" Boris cried. "Tea is . . .
Oh, wait — I will show you."

"This is tea," said Boris. Boris gave Morris
some tea. "Drink it. It will make your throat
feel better."

Morris said, "I am hungry."

"All right," said Boris. "I will make you something to eat. But, first, stick out your tongue."

Morris said, "I will not stick out my tongue. That is not nice."

Boris shouted, "Stick out your tongue!"

Morris stuck out his tongue.

"STOP!" Boris shouted. "That is not nice!"

Morris said, "I told you it was not nice." Boris growled, "That's because you didn't do it the right way."

Boris looked at Morris's tongue. "Oh,"
Boris said. "Your stomach is upset."

Morris asked, "Did you see all the way
down to my stomach?"

"No," said Boris. "I did not see
all the way down to your stomach. I just saw
your tongue. Your tongue is white. When
your tongue is white, it means your stomach
is upset. I know what you should eat. I will
make you some soup."

"Some what?" asked Morris.

"Soup," said Boris. "Soup is —
Oh, wait — I will show you."

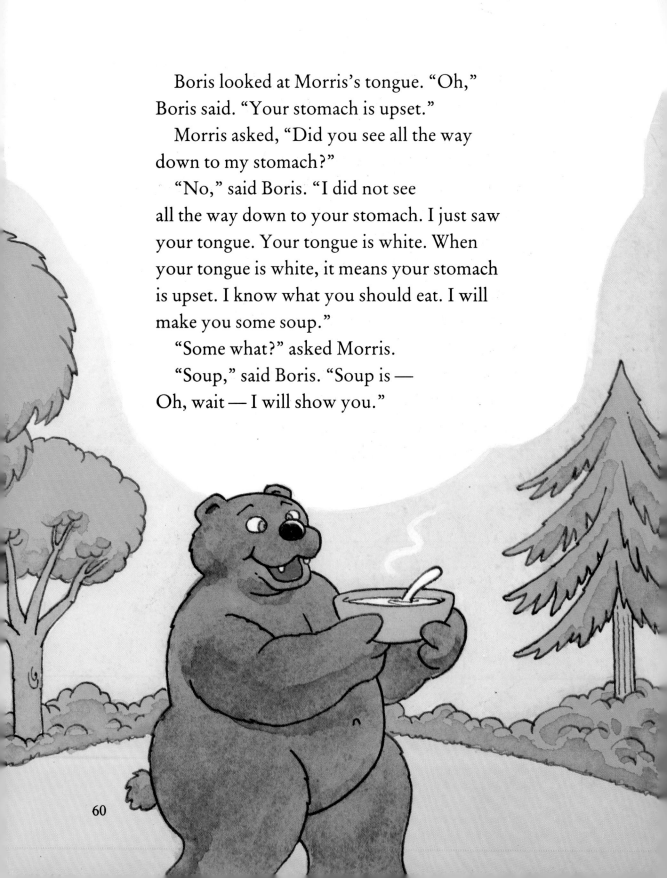

Boris said, "Here is some soup."
Boris fed Morris the soup. Boris ate
some soup, too.

Then Boris said, "It is getting dark.
Go to sleep. If your cold is better in the morning,
I will make you a big breakfast."

"A big what?" Morris asked.

Boris said, "Breakfast. Breakfast is —
Oh! Go to sleep!"

In the morning Morris said, "My nose
is not walking. My one head is not hot.
My cold is better. Make me a big breakfast."

"All right," said Boris. "But
you have to do something for me . . ."

Morris asked, "What?"

"DON'T EVER GET SICK AGAIN!"

How to catch a cold

Colds are very easy to catch — and to share. When a cold-sufferer sneezes, thousands of cold germs are sprayed over anyone unlucky enough to be standing nearby.

If you're stupid enough to like colds, here's how to catch them:

1   Hang around people who don't cover their noses and mouths when they sneeze.
    (Cold germs hate handkerchiefs.)

2   Spend a lot of time in hot stuffy rooms.
    (Cold germs hate fresh air.)

3   Never eat oranges, tomatoes, kiwi fruit, lemons etc.
    (Cold germs hate Vitamin C.)

Words pulled out of a hat

Glossary

absolute silence *(p. 44)*
total silence; not a sound

agreed *(p. 43)*
said it was true or right

audience *(p. 43)*
people watching

cold-sufferer *(p. 62)*
someone who has a cold

eraser *(p. 53)*
rubber

erased *(p. 53)*
rubbed out

forehead *(p. 55)*
the part of the face
above the eyes and
below the hair

moose *(p. 55)*
a large deer, with
very flat antlers

muffler *(p. 51)*
woollen scarf

muttering *(p. 49)*
speaking in a low voice
(sometimes people mutter
when they're angry)

nearby *(p. 62)*
close

nervously *(p. 13)*
feeling worried

Glossary continues on page 64

Morris Morris
I feel sick,
send for the doctor
quick, quick, quick.

Did you hear about
the nut who sneezed?

It was a cashew!

63

pogo stick *(p. 17)*
a jumping stick

porcupine *(p. 42)*
an American animal
with very long, stiff
prickles over its
back and sides

raccoon *(p. 42)*
an American animal
with a long tail and
covered with thick fur

shuffled *(p. 41)*
mixed up the cards

sofa *(p. 49)*
a seat for two or
three people; a settee

sprayed *(p. 62)*
scattered; spread out

students *(p. 40)*
people who are
learning something

tuba *(p. 10)*
a large musical
instrument made
of brass

whipped out *(p. 40)*
pulled out quickly